G0-CDV-377

HEATHCLIFF
CLEANS HOUSE

The funniest feline in America delights millions of fans every day as he appears in over 500 newspapers. You'll have a laugh a minute as Heathcliff tangles with the milkman, the mailman, the veterinarian and just about everyone else he runs into. If you're looking for some fun, look no further. Heathcliff is here.

Heathcliff Books

HEATHCLIFF
HEATHCLIFF RIDES AGAIN
HEATHCLIFF TRIPLE THREAT
HEATHCLIFF WANTED
HEATHCLIFF SPINS A YARN
HEATHCLIFF DOES IT AGAIN!
HEATHCLIFF STRIKES AGAIN!
HEATHCLIFF ROUND 3
HEATHCLIFF PIGS OUT
HEATHCLIFF FIRST PRIZE!
HEATHCLIFF'S TREASURE CHEST OF PUZZLES
HEATHCLIFF'S PUZZLERS
HEATHCLIFF PUZZLE SLEUTH
HEATHCLIFF BANQUET
HEATHCLIFF FEAST
SWEET SAVAGE HEATHCLIFF
WICKED LOVING HEATHCLIFF
HEATHCLIFF IN CONCERT
HEATHCLIFF PLAY BY PLAY
HEATHCLIFF DINES OUT
HEATHCLIFF GONE FISHIN'
HEATHCLIFF CLEANS HOUSE

HEATHCLIFF CLEANS HOUSE

by
Geo Gately

C

CHARTER BOOKS, NEW YORK

Cartoons previously published in
Heathcliff Banquet

HEATHCLIFF CLEANS HOUSE

A Charter Book / published by arrangement with
McNaught Syndicate, Inc.

PRINTING HISTORY
Charter edition / September 1985
Second printing / December 1985

All rights reserved.
Copyright © 1973, 1974, 1980, 1985
by McNaught Syndicate, Inc.
Heathcliff® is a registered trademark
of McNaught Syndicate, Inc.
This book may not be reproduced in whole or in part,
by mimeograph or any other means, without permission.
For information address: The Berkley Publishing Group,
200 Madison Avenue, New York, New York 10016.

ISBN: 0-441-32248-4

Charter Books are published by The Berkley Publishing Group,
200 Madison Avenue, New York, New York 10016.
PRINTED IN THE UNITED STATES OF AMERICA

WHEN IT ALL BEGAN . . . →

SEPTEMBER 3ʳᵈ, 1973
THE FIRST 'HEATHCLIFF' CARTOON!

"He's a winner!" . . . Many reasons have been given for Heathcliff's popularity, but this seems to sum it up best. Through the years, cats have been depicted as either sinister or stupid, neither of which is true. Cats are smart! And so is Heathcliff! As you look through this book, you'll see how Heathcliff has evolved from the very first day through the years . . . Enjoy!

"A VANILLA FUDGE SUNDAE AND A RAW FISH."

"WATCH THIS, GRAMPS...."

"HEATHCLIFF KNOWS THE EXACT LENGTH
OF THAT LEASH!"

"WHAT HAPPENED TO HEATHCLIFF'S
SCRATCHING POST?!"

© 1973 McNaught Synd., Inc.
Geo Gately
9-6

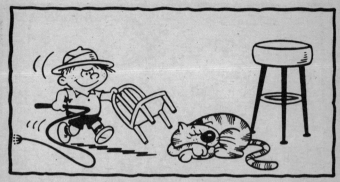

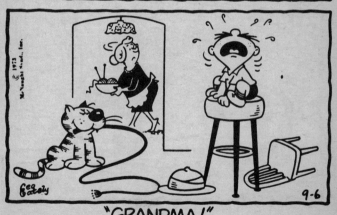

"GRANDMA!"

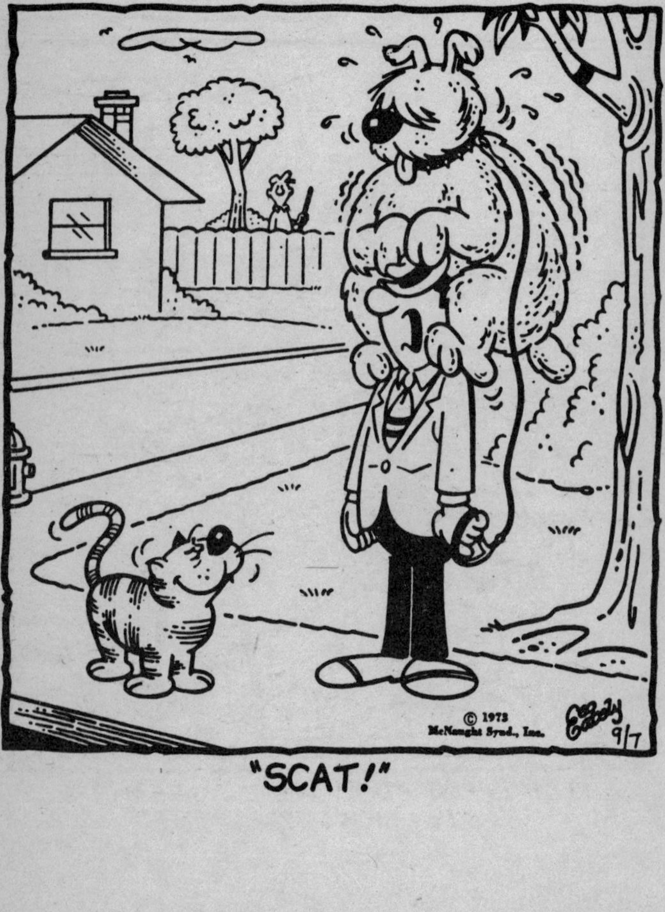
© 1973
McNaught Synd., Inc.
9/7

"SCAT!"

"PLUS TWENTY DOLLARS DAMAGE IN THE
FROZEN FISH DEPARTMENT!"

"YOU'RE SITTING ON HIS DEAD MOUSE."

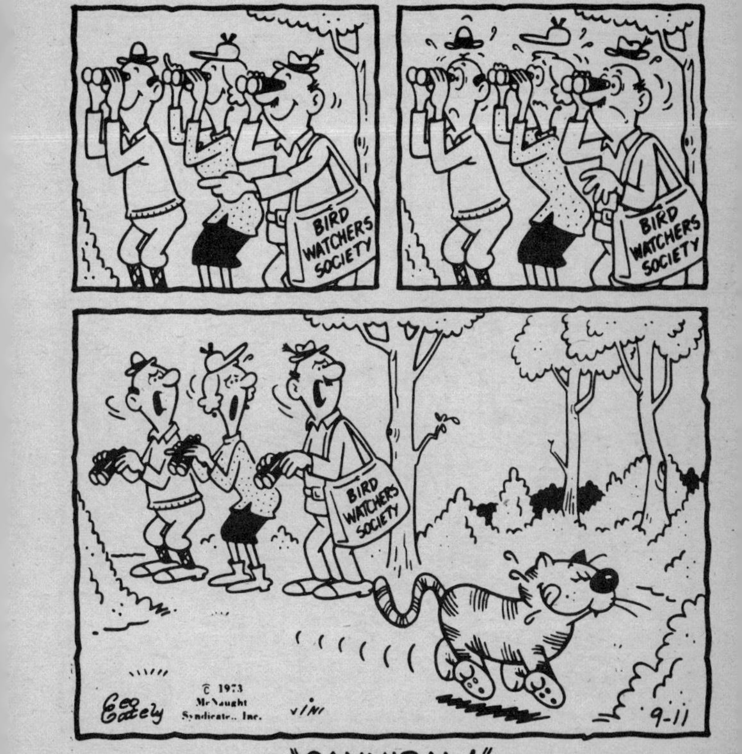
BIRD WATCHERS SOCIETY
BIRD WATCHERS SOCIETY
BIRD WATCHERS SOCIETY
Geo Gately
© 1973 McNaught Syndicate, Inc.
9-11

"CANNIBAL!"

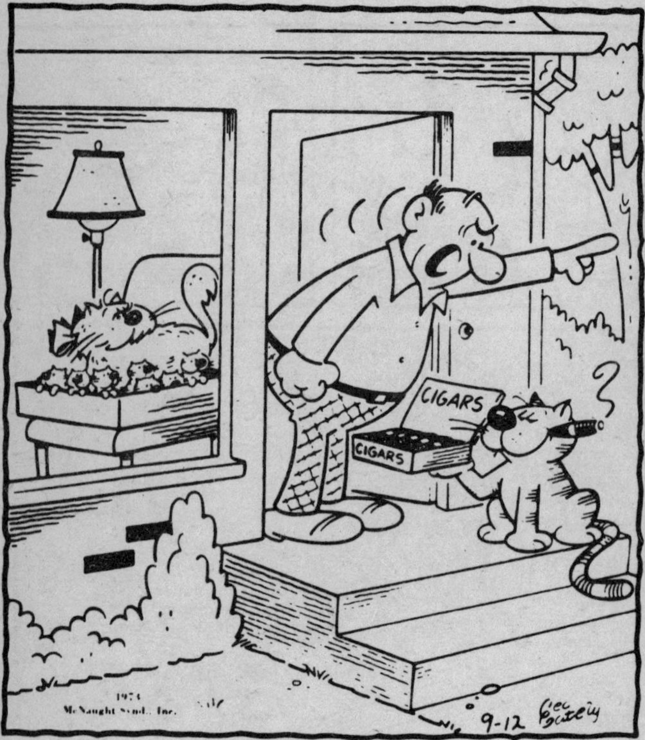
CIGARS
CIGARS
?
9-12

"GET LOST!"

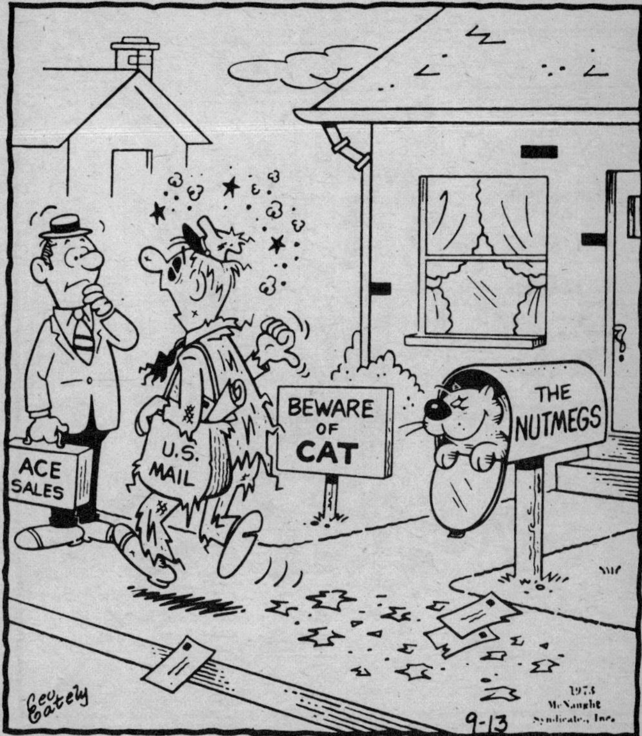
ACE
SALES
U.S.
MAIL
BEWARE
OF
CAT
THE
NUTMEGS
Geo Eately
9-13
1973
McNaught
Syndicate, Inc.

"YOU'D BETTER BELIEVE IT!"

"HEATHCLIFF HAS BEEN A VERY NAUGHTY
PUSSY CAT TODAY."

" I COULD HAVE SWORN SOMEONE TRIPPED ME !"

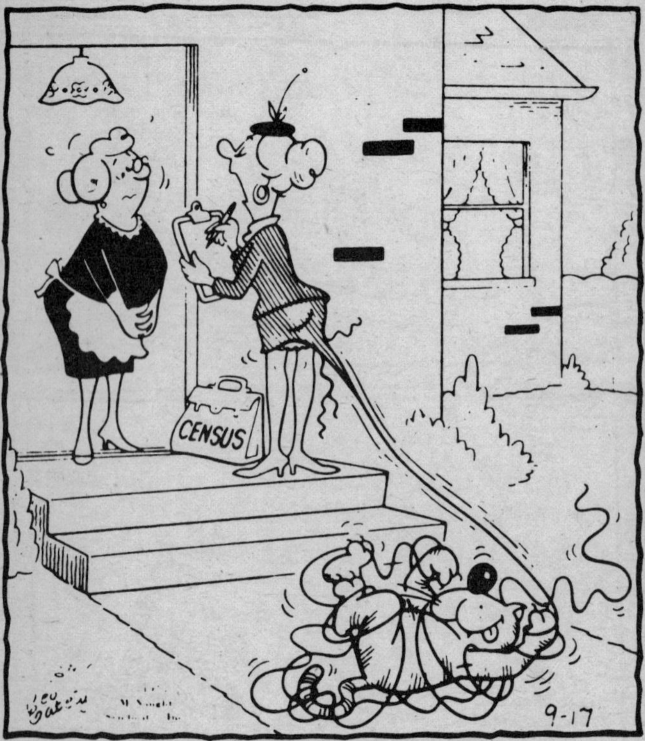
CENSUS
9-17

"ANY PETS?"

"YOU SAY YOU FOUND A LARGE, STRIPED, CANTANKEROUS TOM-CAT..."

"FINDERS KEEPERS!"

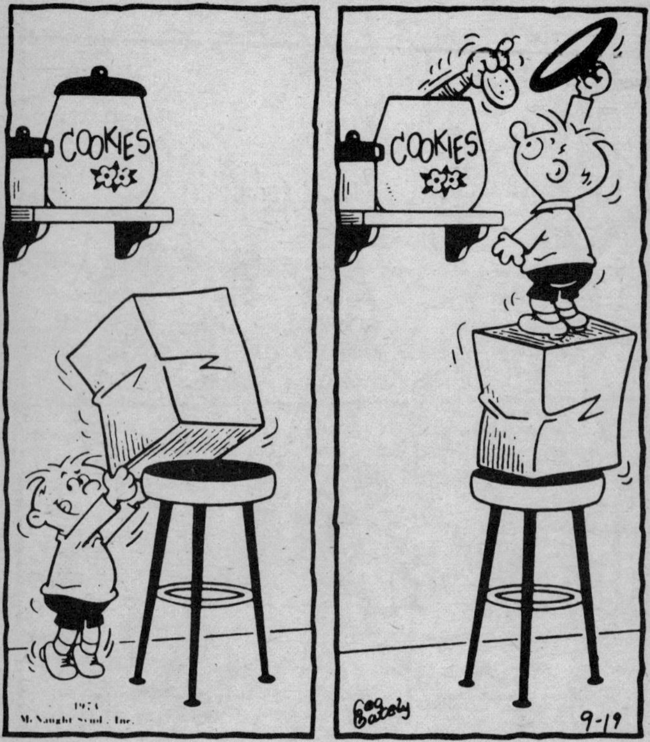
COOKIES
COOKIES
9-19

"YOU MUST HAVE CAUGHT SOMETHING."

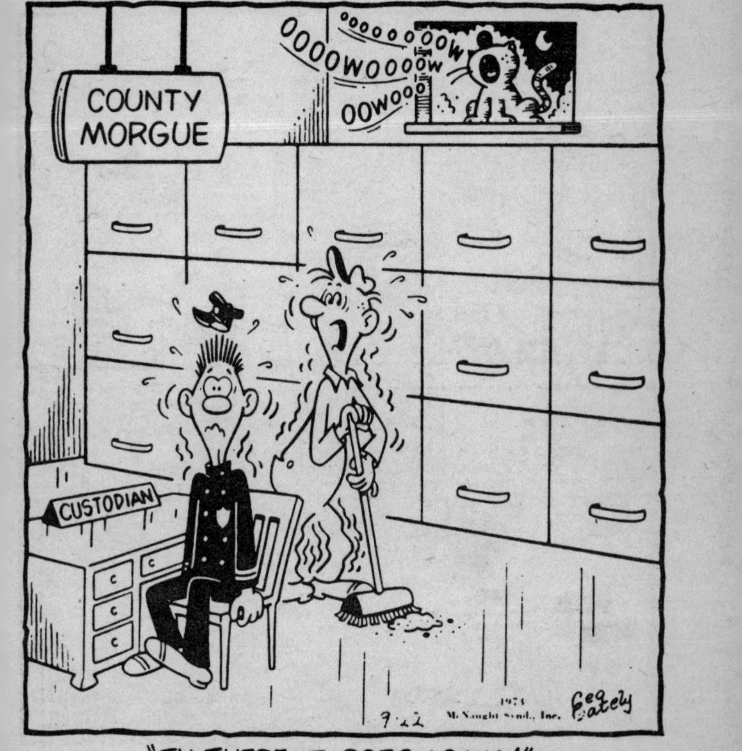
COUNTY
MORGUE
CUSTODIAN

"TH-THERE IT GOES AGAIN!"

"THAT ALWAYS MAKES HIS DAY."

"HEATHCLIFF JUST LOVES IT WHEN I PLAY
'KITTEN ON THE KEYS'."

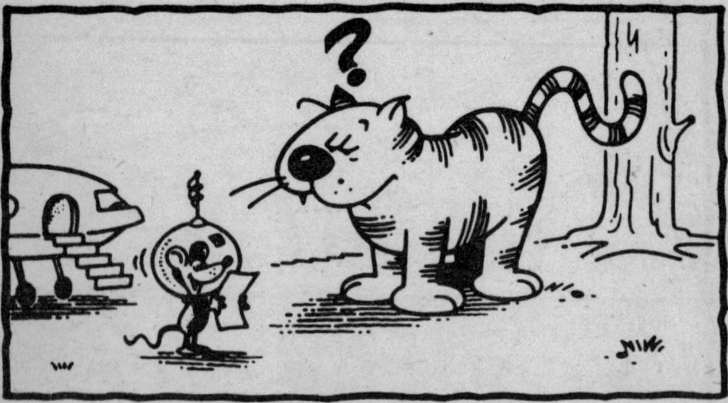

"GREETINGS, EARTHLING...."

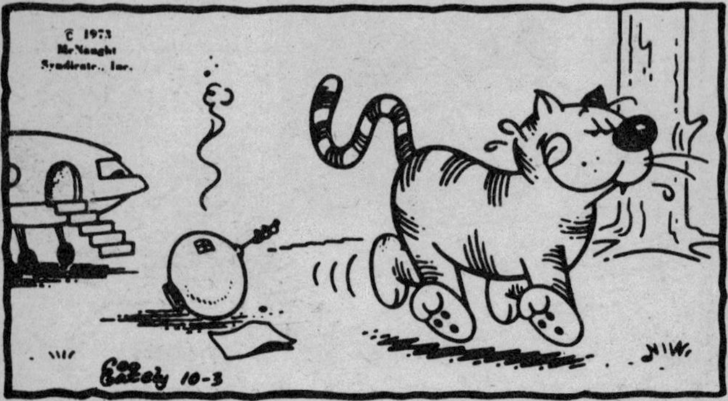
© 1973
McNaught
Syndicate., Inc.
10-3

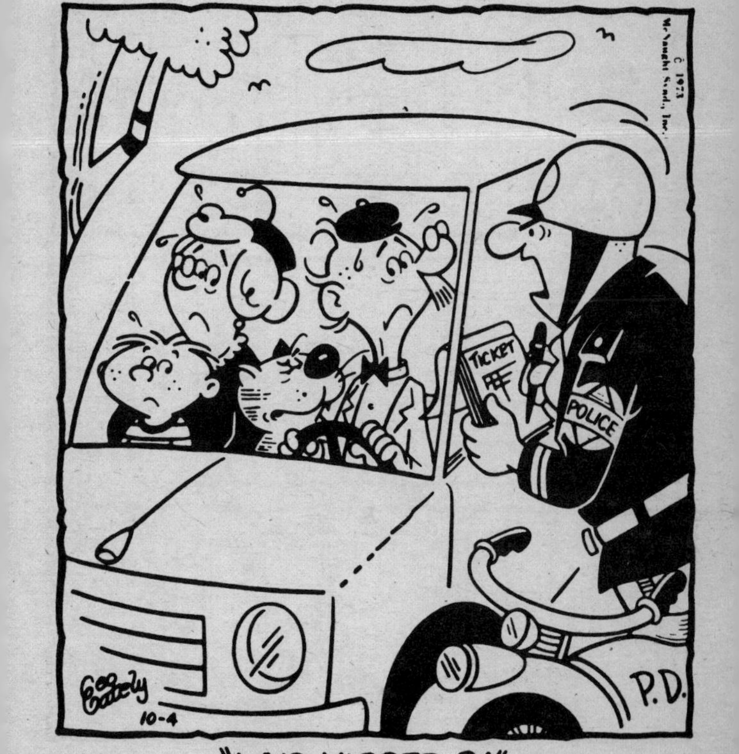
© 1973 McNaught Synd., Inc.
TICKET
POLICE
Geo Gately
10-4
P.D.

"WHO HISSED ?!"

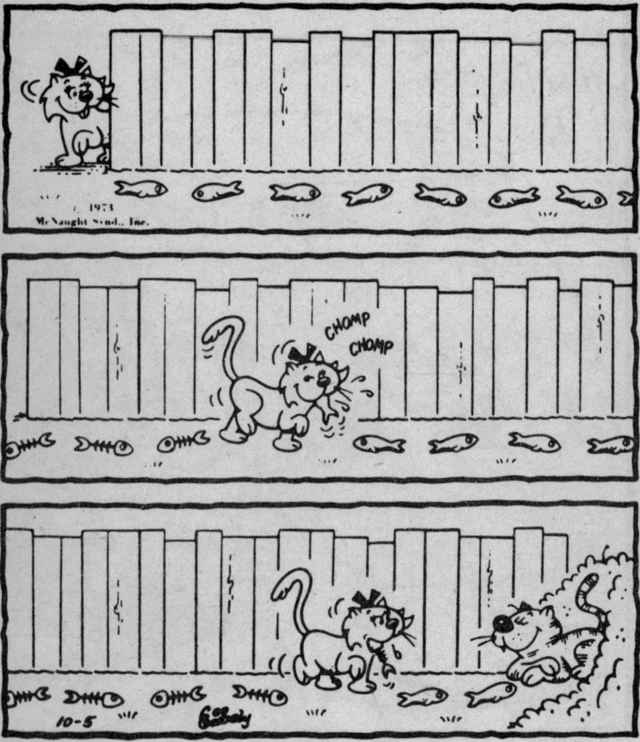
© 1973
McNaught Synd., Inc.
CHOMP
CHOMP
10-5

"HE'LL CLIMB JUST ABOUT ANYTHING."

"I LAID OUT YOUR GOOD SUIT
ON THE BED, DEAR."

"THIS SHOULD BE INTERESTING."

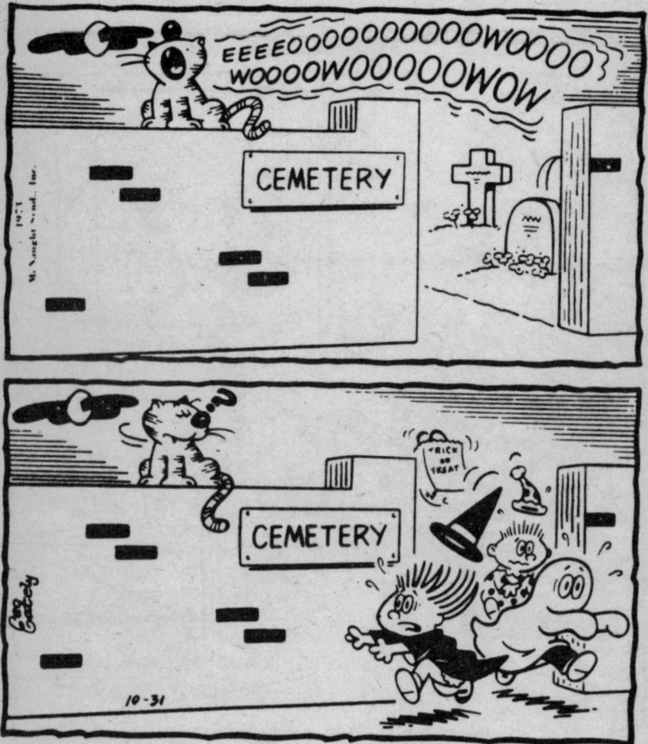
EEEEOOOOOOOOOOWOOOO
WOOOOWOOOOOWOW
CEMETERY
CEMETERY
TRICK OR TREAT
10-31

"IT'S A LIST OF COMPLAINTS ABOUT
HEATHCLIFF FROM THE NEIGHBORS."

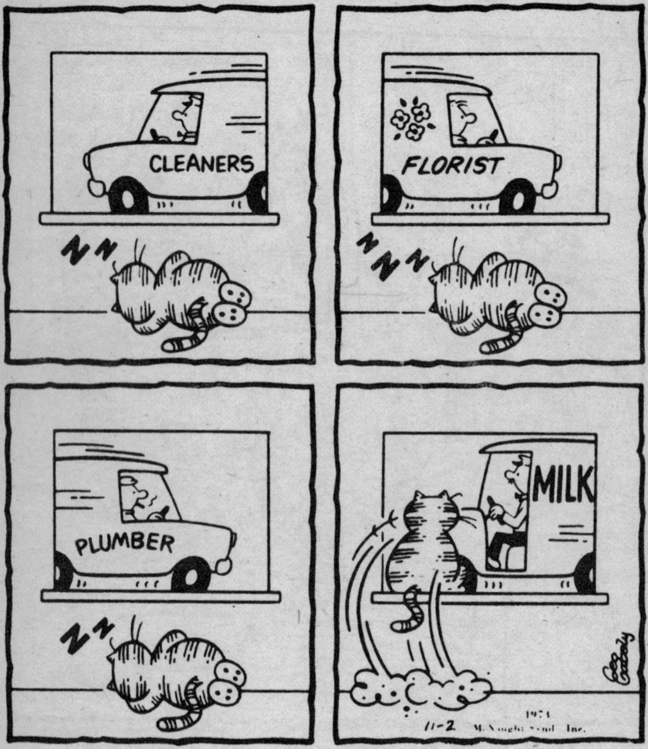
CLEANERS
FLORIST
PLUMBER
MILK
11-2
1978 McNaught Synd. Inc.

"BETTER KEEP AN EYE ON THOSE TWO."

"LISTEN!...THERE IT GOES AGAIN!"

"HEAVENS! WHO MADE SUCH A MESS?"

"GUESS?"

"GOD BLESS GRANDMA, GOD BLESS GRANDPA, AND GOD FORGIVE HEATHCLIFF."

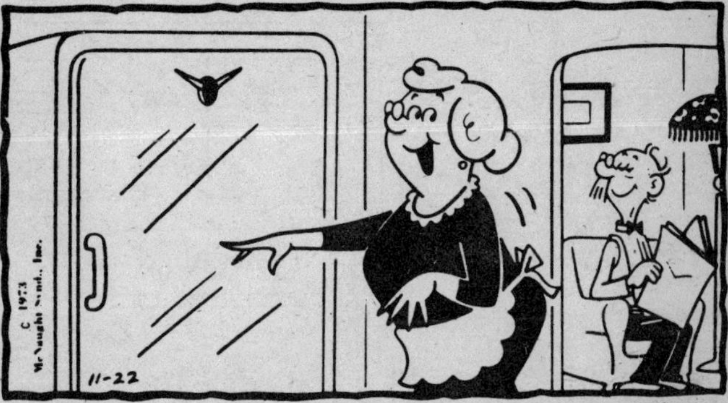
11-22

"HOW ABOUT A NICE TURKEY SANDWICH?"

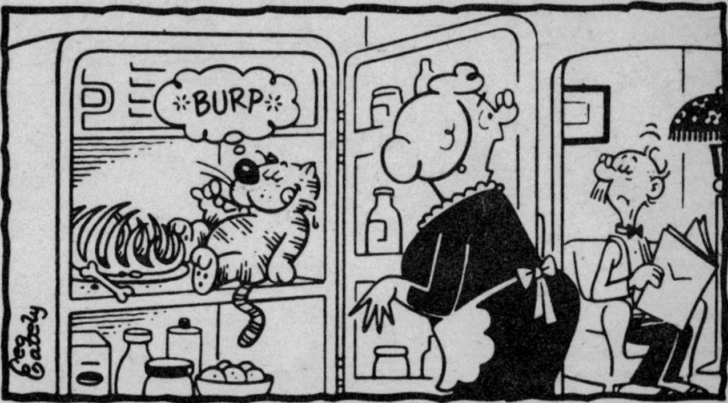
BURP

"WOULD YOU SETTLE FOR A
PEANUT BUTTER AND JELLY?"

"I TELL YOU THERE WAS A WHOLE STACK
OF TWENTIES HERE A MOMENT AGO!"

McNaught
11-27

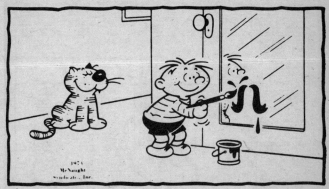

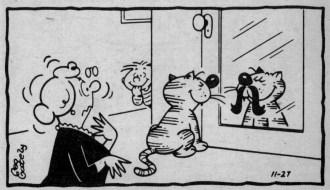

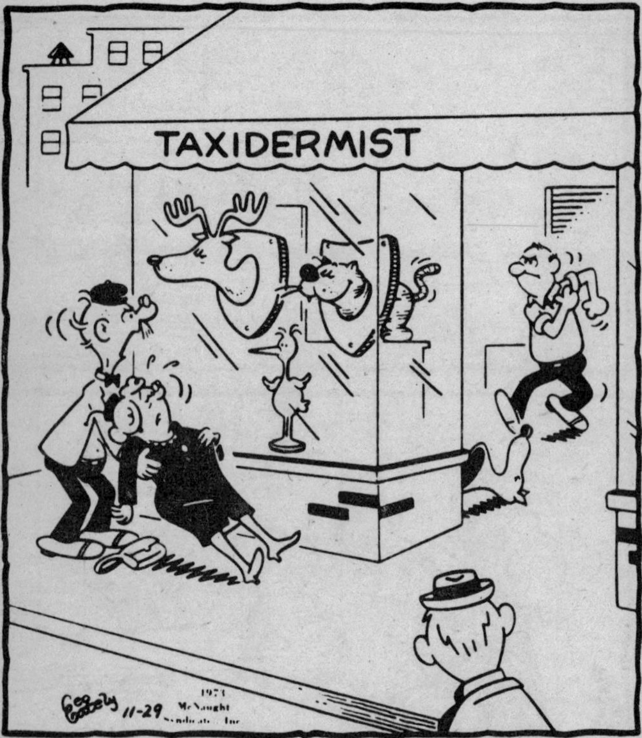
TAXIDERMIST
11-29
1973 McNaught Syndicate, Inc.

"NOW CUT THAT OUT!"

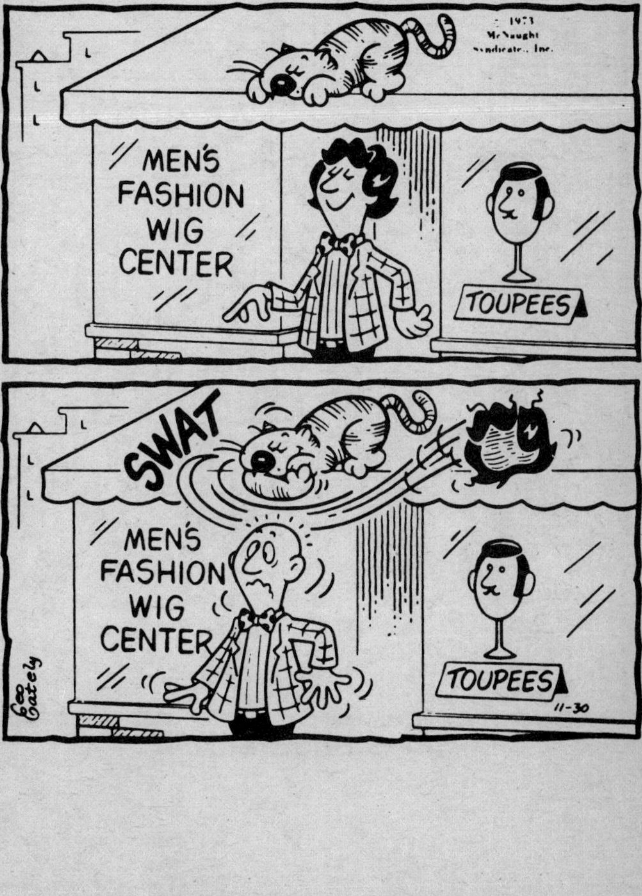
1973
McNaught
Syndicate, Inc.
MEN'S
FASHION
WIG
CENTER
TOUPEES
SWAT
MEN'S
FASHION
WIG
CENTER
TOUPEES
Geo Gately
11-30

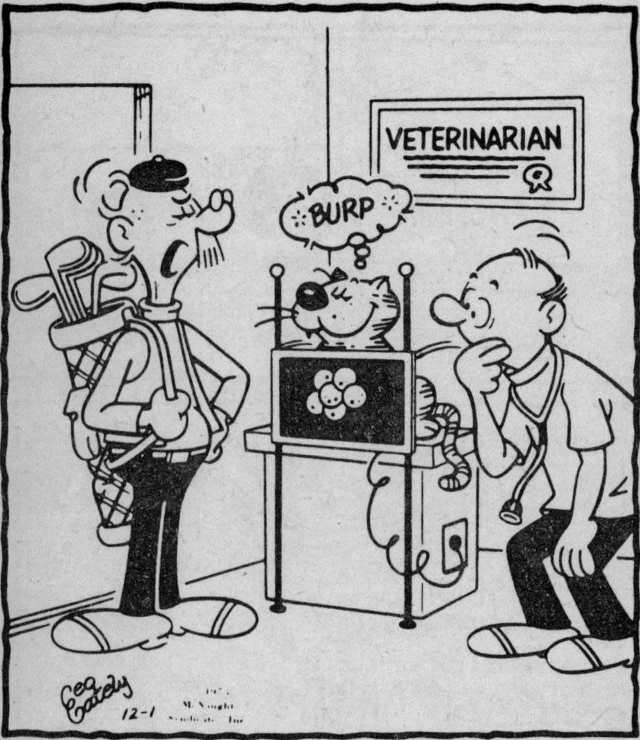
VETERINARIAN
BURP

"JUST AS I SUSPECTED!"

"WHAT HAPPENED TO MY MISTLETOE?"

"GUESS WHO HAS BEEN ACCUSED
OF BEING A CHICKEN THIEF?"

"ANY MESSAGES FOR LOVER BOY?"

FOOTBALL
STADIUM
Z Z Z
11-23
1973 McNaught Synd., Inc.
FOOTBALL
STADIUM
12
Gately

"WELL, SO MUCH FOR THE GUARANTEED
INDESTRUCTIBLE CAT TOYS."

"OH, THAT'S JUST HEATHCLIFF YAWNING."

MEOOW!
DOG SHOW
JUDGE
DOG SHOW
DISQUALIFIED
12-27
McNaught Synd., Inc.

"DO YOU THINK HE ATE THE WHOLE THING?"

"PRETTY SNEAKY WAY TO CATCH BIRDS,
IF YOU ASK ME."

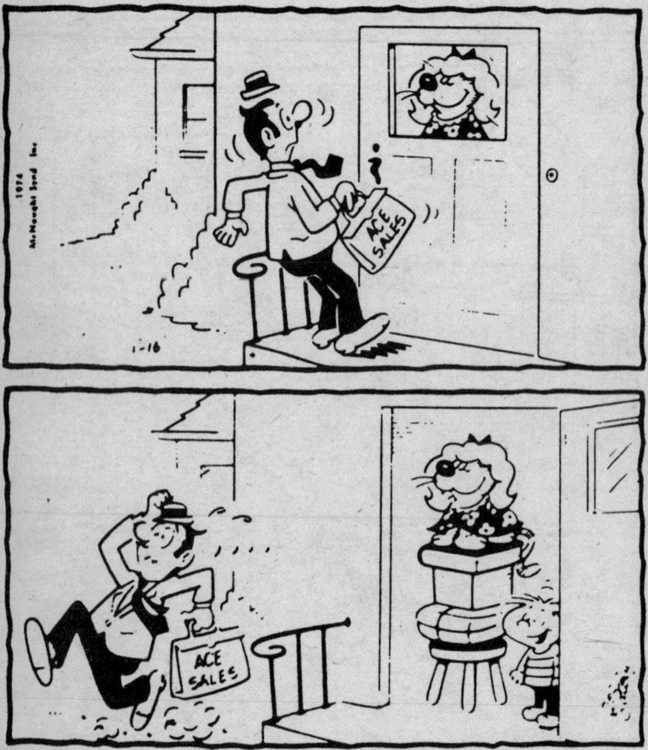
ACE SALES
1-16
ACE SALES

"IT WORKED!"

"HOW ABOUT THAT!... I FINALLY MADE IT
TO THE MILK BOX WITHOUT RUNNING
INTO HEATHCLIFF."

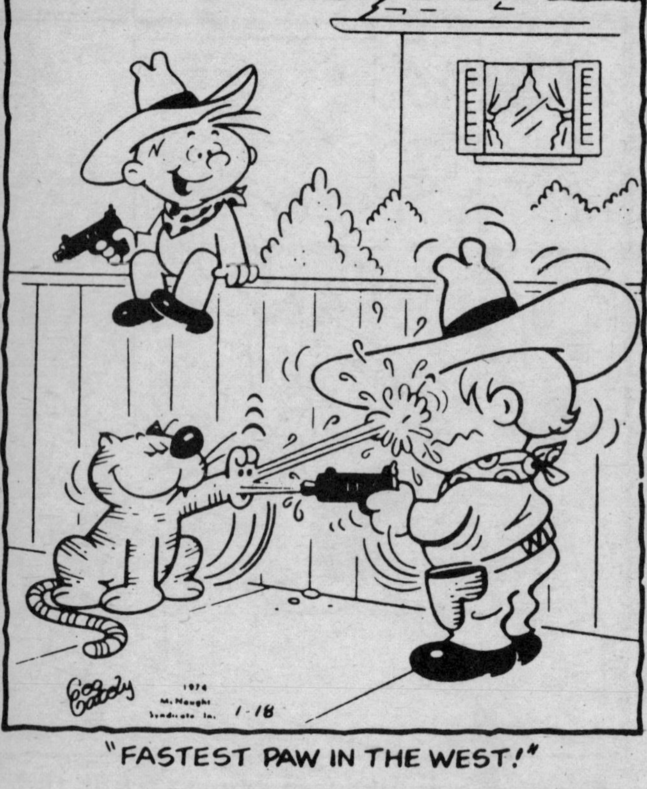
1-18

"FASTEST PAW IN THE WEST!"

"I DON'T KNOW...HE WAS RIGHT HERE
A MOMENT AGO!"

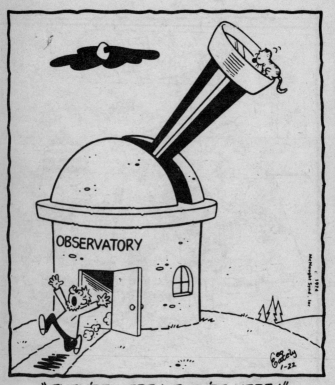

"THEY'RE HERE! THEY'RE HERE!"

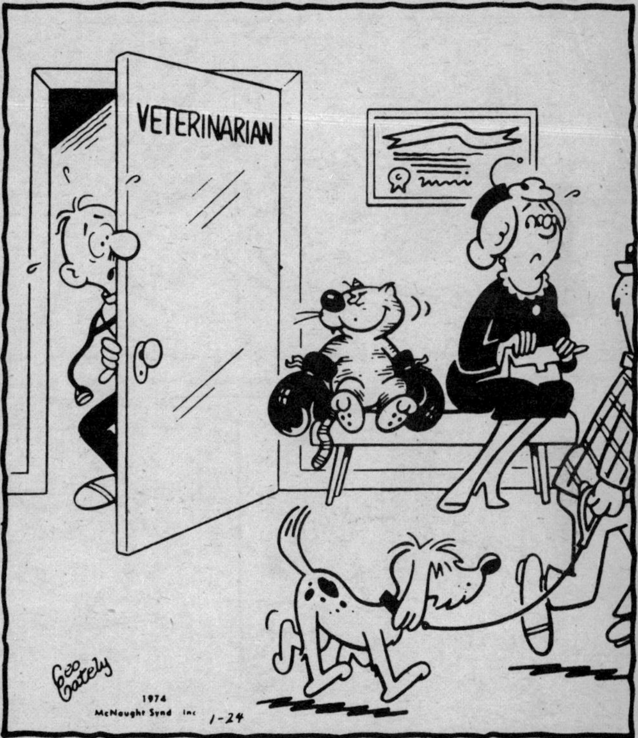
VETERINARIAN
Geo Gately
1974
McNaught Synd Inc
1-24

"ER.... NEXT."

"I GUESS THIS MEANS WE CAN'T KEEP HIM, HEATHCLIFF."

"I THINK HE'S HOPING WE WON'T NOTICE."

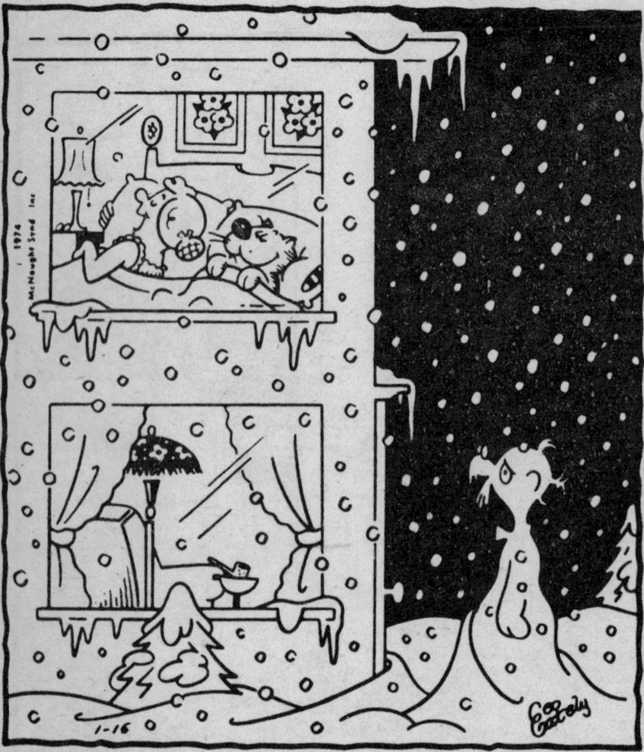
1-16

"I DON'T KNOW WHY YOU ALWAYS MAKE SUCH A FUSS ABOUT PUTTING HEATHCLIFF OUT FOR THE NIGHT."

"HEATHCLIFF TOOK FIRST PRIZE AT THE PET SHOW!"

"HE TOOK IT FROM THE CAT THAT WON IT."

"TELL ME, HOW DOES AN ELECTRIC BLANKET JUST UP AND DISAPPEAR?"

"NO, NO, HEATHCLIFF... MUSTN'T TOUCH!"

"IT'S ONE OF THOSE WHISTLES THAT ONLY
DOGS CAN HEAR."

" THE CLAM CHOWDER IS DELICIOUS TODAY..."

" WASN'T IT ?! "

"JUST THINK, WE'LL BE THE FIRST ONES TO EVER MAKE IT TO THE TOP OF THIS MOUNTAIN!"

"LOOK OUT!...HERE COMES THE GOURMET!"

"HEATHCLIFF JUST LOVES TO SHOW OFF
HIS STRING COLLECTION."

©1974 McNaught Synd. Inc
MILK
COINS
MILK
1-23
MILK
COINS
MILK
MILK

"I WOULDN'T GO NEAR
THAT TREE, IF I WERE YOU."

"I WARNED YOU."

"I COULD HAVE SWORN I JUST OPENED
A CAN OF SARDINES!"

"NOW REMEMBER, WHEN I CALL
HEATHCLIFF OUT, LET HIM HAVE IT!"

"YOU LOVE TO CHASE MICE, EAT FISH AND
RUMMAGE THROUGH GARBAGE CANS."

"EVER HAVE YOUR WHOLE LIFE PASS BEFORE YOU ?!"

"HEATHCLIFF GOT A PRIZE FOR LEAVING
THE PARTY EARLY."

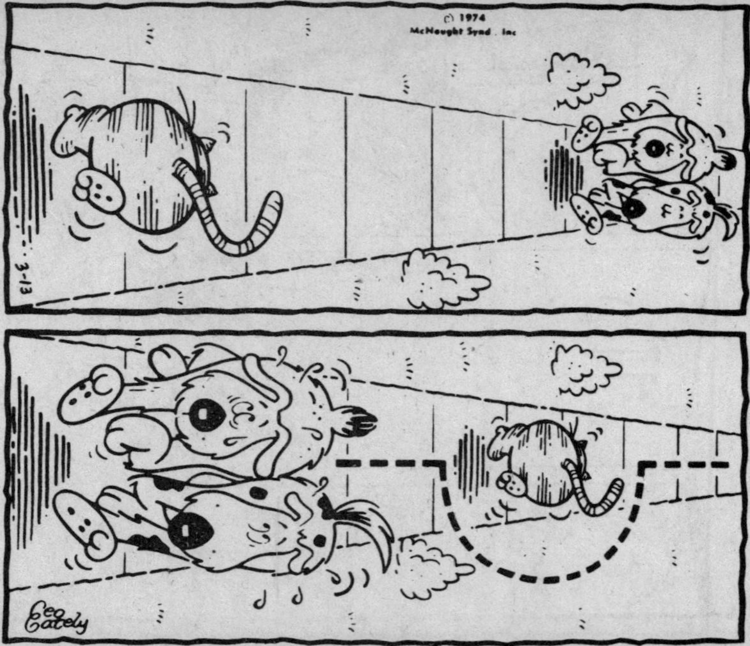
© 1974
McNaught Synd. Inc
3-13
Leo Gately

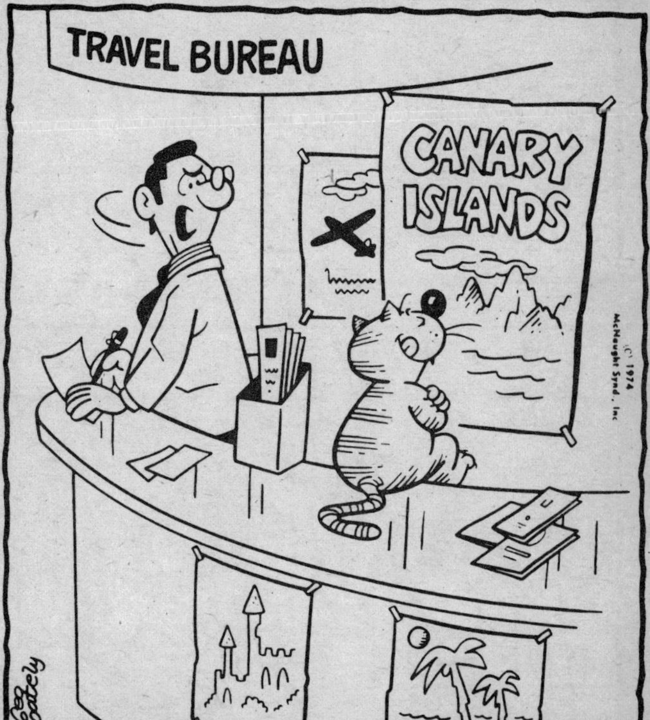
TRAVEL BUREAU
CANARY ISLANDS
(C) 1974 McNaught Synd., Inc
3-14

"YOU AGAIN ?!"

"MRS. NUTMEG, HAVE YOU SEEN LUDWIG, MY PET CANARY?"

"DO THEY HAVE ANYTHING THAT WILL *SAP* HIS ENERGY?"

"THAT'S THE FIRST TIME I'VE GOTTEN THROUGH THIS NEIGHBORHOOD WITHOUT RUNNING INTO HEATHCLIFF!"

"UMMM...HEH, HEH...HE ALWAYS COULD FIND THE MOST COMFORTABLE CHAIR IN THE HOUSE."

"OTHER CATS JUST LEAVE THEIR FOOTPRINTS!"

"HURRY UP!...SHE'S TIRED OF WAITING!"

"HOW ABOUT A MIDNIGHT...

...SNACK?"

"...AND WE GUARANTEE RESULTS!"

"CAT FOOD COMMERCIALS ARE UNLISTED."

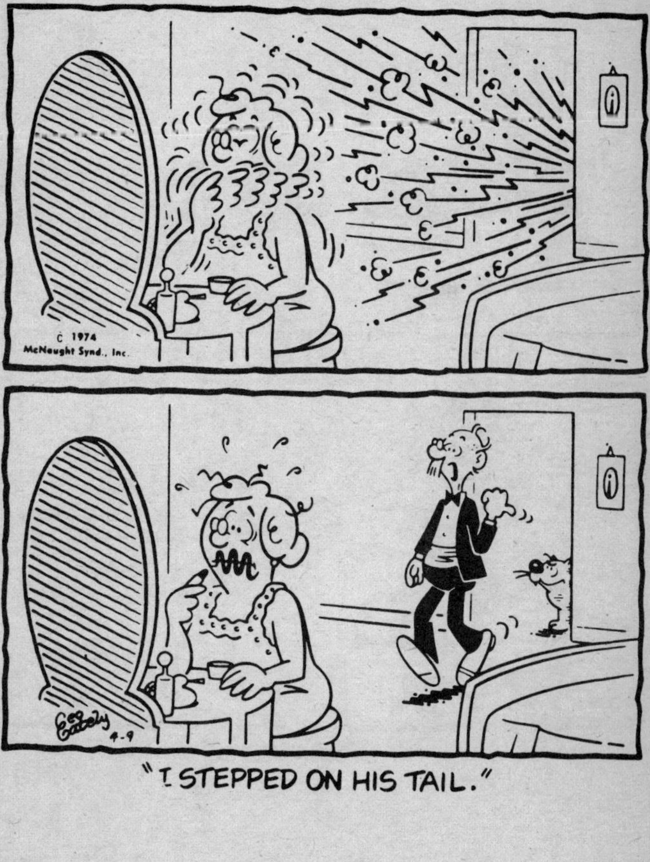
© 1974
McNaught Synd., Inc.

"I STEPPED ON HIS TAIL."

" THERE... NOW, LET ME HAVE THE...

...CREAM!"

C. 1974
McNaught Synd., Inc

SPLAT

"ALL OUT FOR THE
EASTER EGG HUNT!"

"WALDO, GET IN HERE!...DON'T YOU KNOW
ENOUGH TO COME IN OUT OF THE RAIN?"

"CAUGHT HIM WITH HIS HAND IN THE COOKIE JAR AGAIN!"

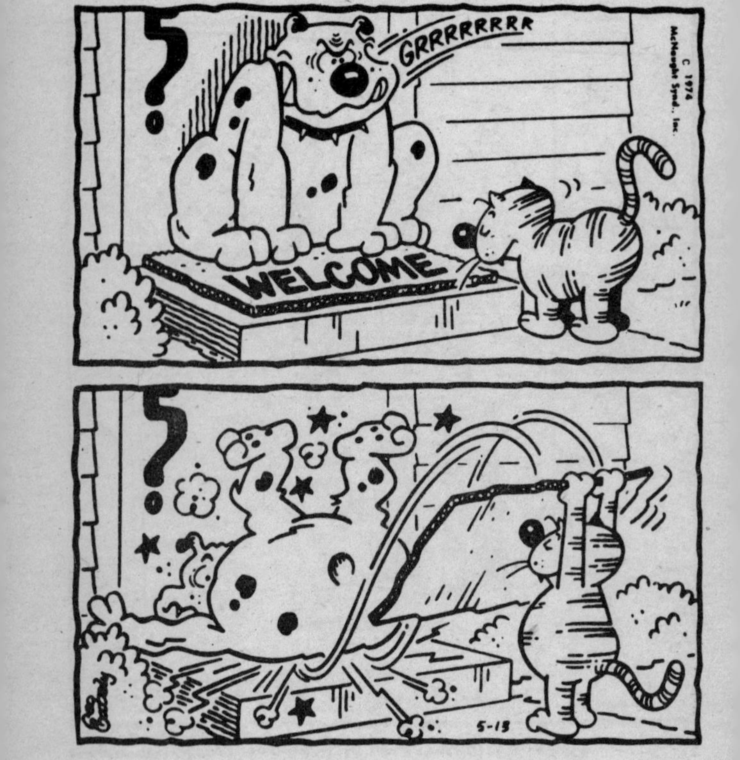
5
GRRRRRRRR
C 1974
McNaught Synd., Inc.
WELCOME
5
5-13

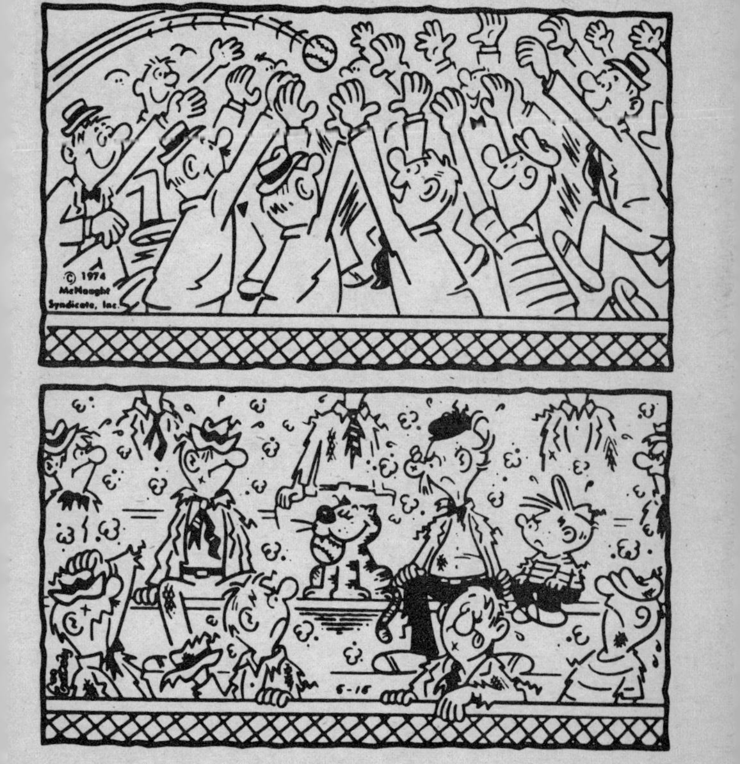
© 1974
McNaught
Syndicate, Inc.
6-16

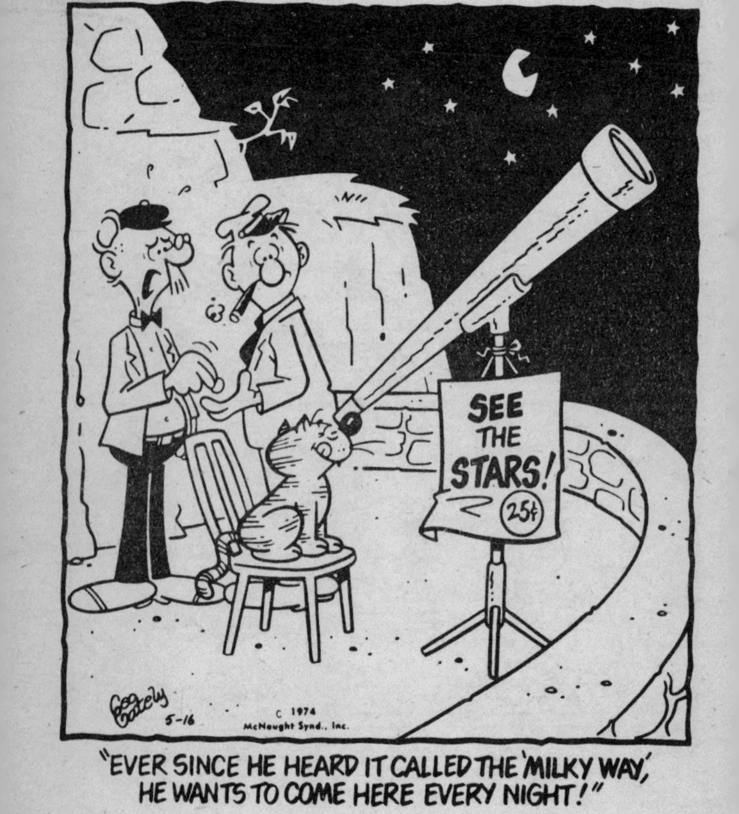
SEE THE STARS!
25¢
5-16
c 1974
McNaught Synd., Inc.
"EVER SINCE HE HEARD IT CALLED THE 'MILKY WAY,' HE WANTS TO COME HERE EVERY NIGHT!"

"HE REACHED OVER THE SIDE OF THE BOAT
AND SWATTED IT."

"IT'S HEATHCLIFF AND FRIEND, PERFORMING IN STEREO."

"HEY! WHAT ARE YOU DOING WITH MY HAT?"

"MAYBE WE COULD TRADE HIM YOUR PET
GOLDFISH!"

"REALLY?!... WELL, THAT'S THE FIRST FIGHT
HEATHCLIFF EVER LOST TO A PUSSYCAT!"

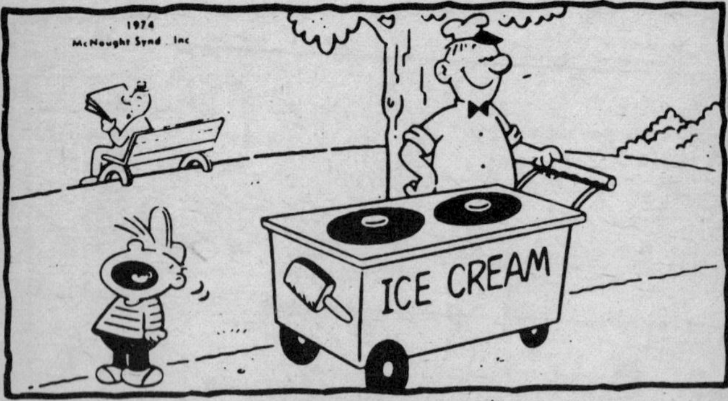
1974
McNaught Synd. Inc
ICE CREAM

"HEATHCLIFF!"

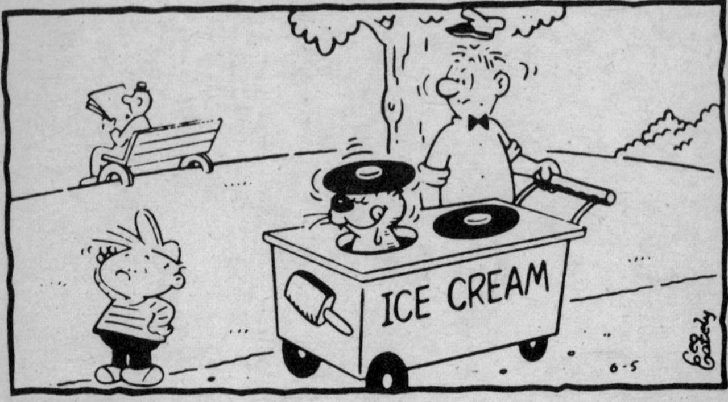
ICE CREAM
6-5

"HEATHCLIFF WOULD LIKE IT GIFT WRAPPED."

"SAY EDDIE, DID YOU HEAR A ROAR?!"

"HERE'S ONE THAT SOUNDS GOOD...
'NO PETS ALLOWED'."

"DID YOU ACTUALLY *SEE* HEATHCLIFF
IN YOUR FLOWER BED?"

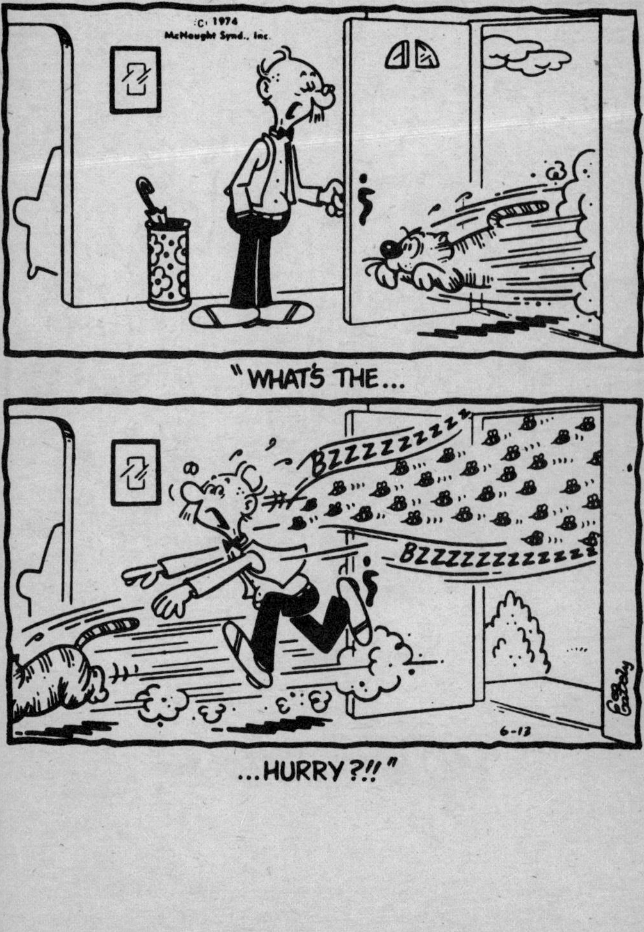
©1974
McNaught Synd., Inc.
"WHAT'S THE...
BZZZZZZZZZZ
BZZZZZZZZZZZZZZ
6-13
...HURRY?!!"

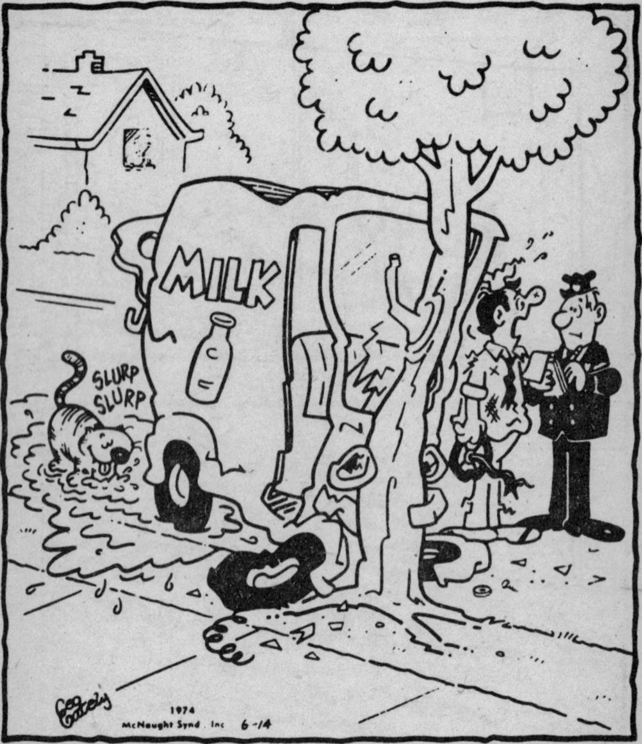
MILK
SLURP
SLURP
1974
McNaught Synd. Inc
6-14

"A CAT RAN IN FRONT OF ME!"

"GAME CALLED ON ACCOUNT OF *CHEWED UP BALL!*"

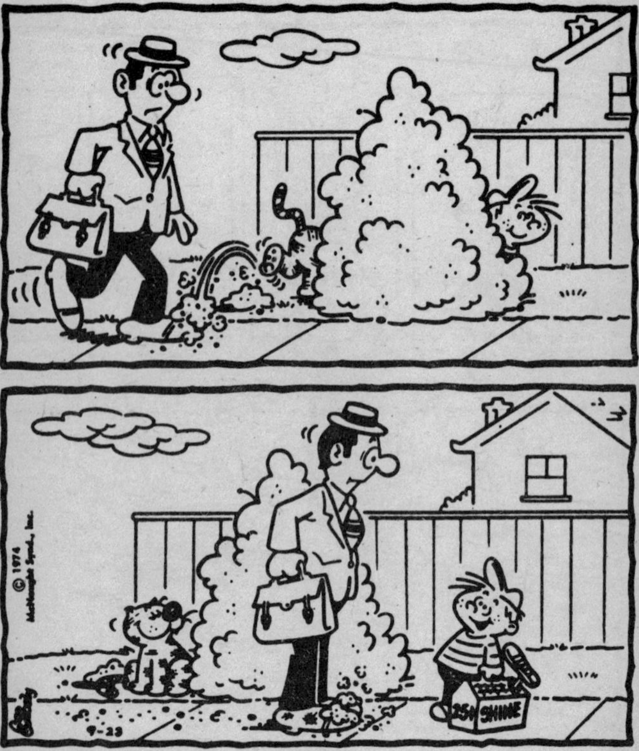
© 1974 McNaught Synd., Inc.
9-23
25¢ SHINE

"SHINE ?"

"WHAT? LOST YOUR MITTENS? YOU *NAUGHTY* KITTENS,
THEN YOU SHALL HAVE NO PIE!"

"BOY, I'D HATE TO BE A MOUSE THIS MORNING!"

"HE LIKES TO CATERWAUL BY THE MYSTERY SECTION."

"I'D LIKE YOU TO MEET HEATHCLIFF II, HEATHCLIFF III,
HEATHCLIFF IV, HEATHCLIFF V...."

"HE JUST SCARED THE SPOTS OFF A DALMATIAN!"

"THE GRIEVANCE COMMITTEE IS HERE TO SEE YOU."

© 1974
McNaught Synd., Inc.

"OUT!"

"DON'T HAND OFF TO HEATHCLIFF...
YOU'LL NEVER SEE THE BALL AGAIN!"

"SOMEONE LICKED ALL THE TRADING STAMPS!"

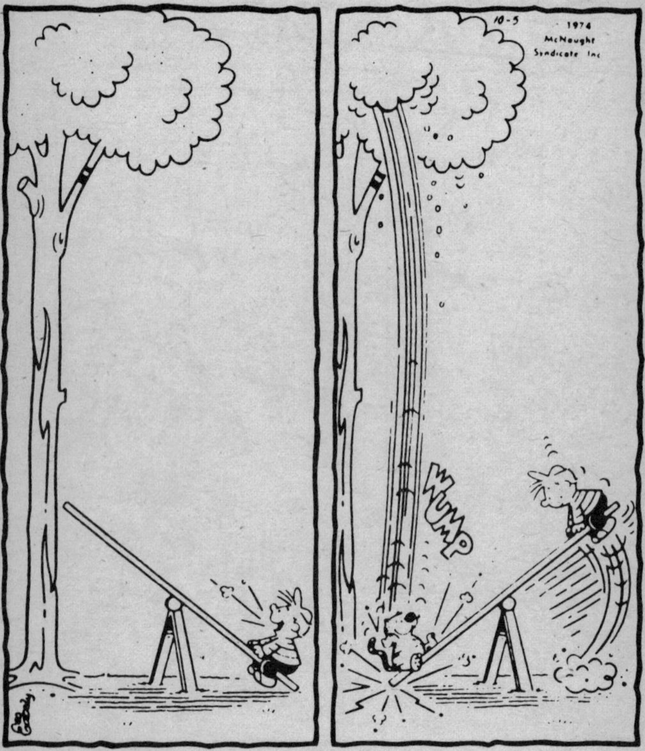
WUMP
10-5
1974 McNaught Syndicate Inc

"NOW!"

"YOU'LL BE GLAD TO KNOW HEATHCLIFF GOT DOWN
OFF THE ROOF ALL BY HIMSELF."

PROPERTY OF
BUGGSY FABER
RIP
"HAH! TRICK OR TREAT, CAT!"
1974
McNaught Synd., Inc
10-30
PROPERTY OF

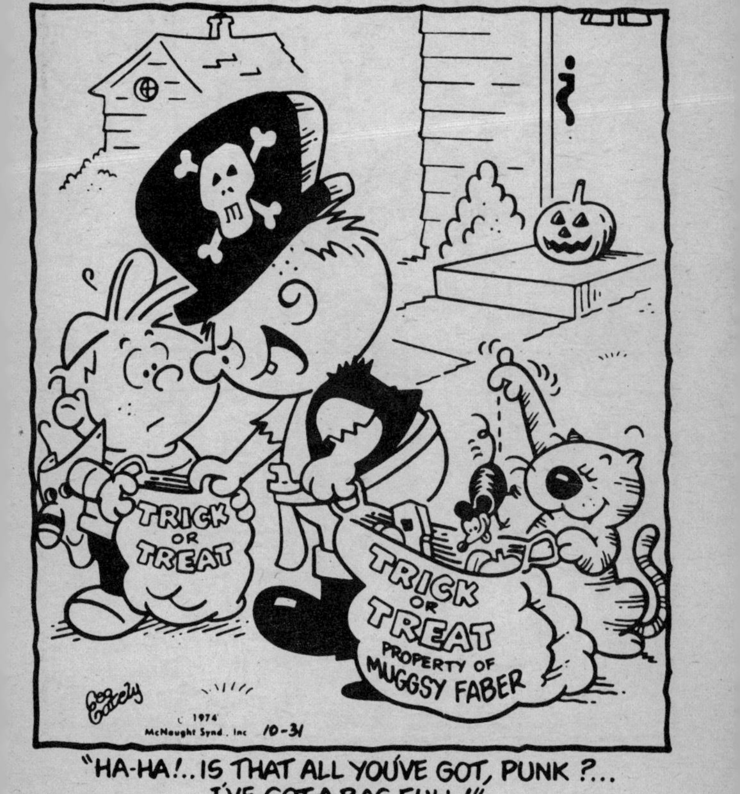
TRICK
OR
TREAT
TRICK
OR
TREAT
PROPERTY OF
MUGGSY FABER
© 1974
McNaught Synd., Inc
10-31

"HA-HA!.. IS THAT ALL YOU'VE GOT, PUNK ?...
I'VE GOT A BAG FULL!"

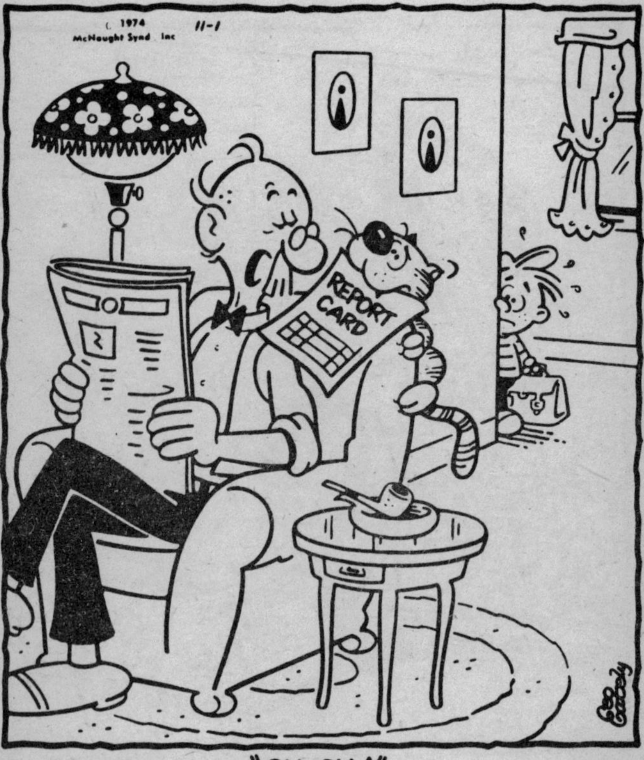
© 1974 McNaught Synd. Inc
11-1
REPORT CARD

"OH, OH!"

"HE FINALLY DID IT!...HE HIT HIGH `C`!"

"I WANT TO INTERVIEW THE ROUGHEST, TOUGHEST BRUISER ON THE SQUAD!"

"THESE ARE LOVABLE, WELL-BEHAVED PUSSYCATS...
...NOTHING LIKE THEIR FATHER!"

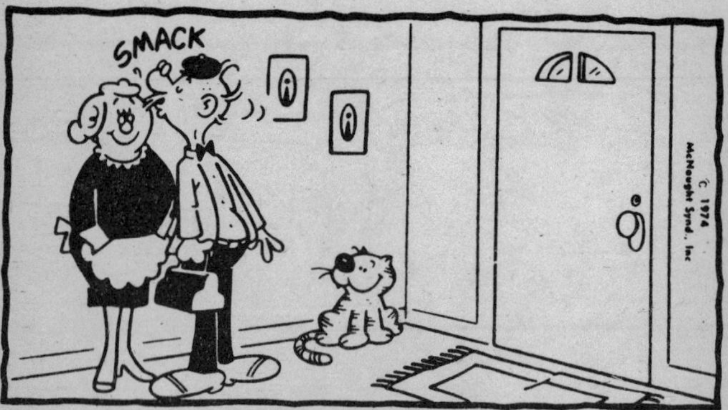
SMACK
© 1974 McNaught Synd., Inc

"GOODBYE, DEAR."

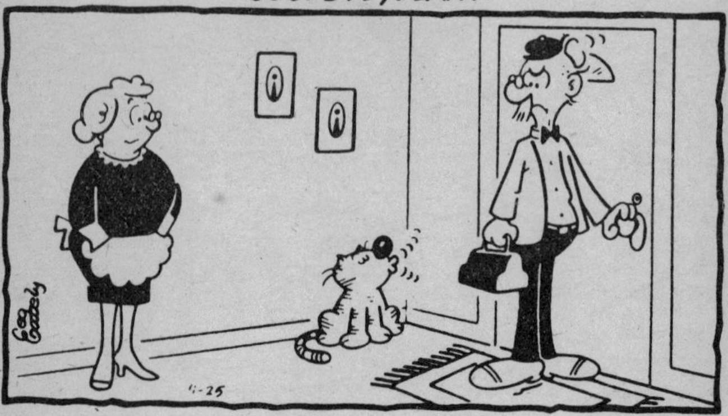